SUPERDOODLES

DINOSAURS

WRITTEN AND ILLUSTRATED BY BEV ARMSTRONG

The Learning Works

The Learning Works

Designed and edited by
Sherri M. Butterfield

Copyright © 1993
The Learning Works, Inc.
Santa Barbara, California 93160

Library of Congress Catalog Number: 92-074102
ISBN 0-88160-223-X
LW 301

Printed in the United States of America.

Current Printing (last digit):
10 9 8 7 6 5 4 3 2 1

Introduction

SUPERDOODLES are books that provide simple, step-by-step instructions for super line drawings. The creatures in this book may be sketched large for murals or posters, or small for bookmarks and flip books. They may be used individually in separate pictures or combined to create a prehistoric panorama.

As you follow the steps, draw in pencil. Dotted lines appear in some steps. Make these lines light so that they can be easily erased later. When you have finished your drawing, erase all unnecessary lines. To give your drawing a finished look, go over the remaining lines with a colored pencil, crayon, or felt-tipped pen.

If you enjoy this book, look for other **Learning Works SUPERDOODLES.** Titles in this series include *Mammals, Rain Forest, Sports,* and *Vehicles.*

allosaurus

35 feet long

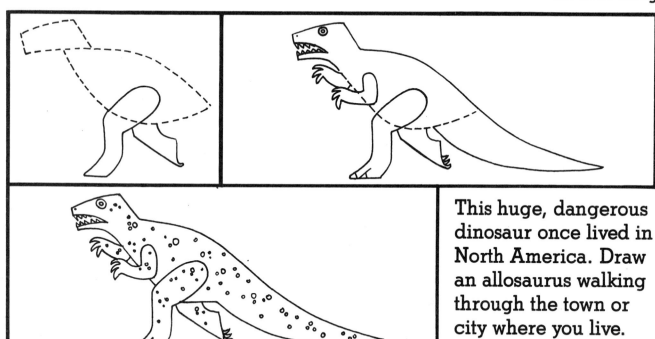

This huge, dangerous dinosaur once lived in North America. Draw an allosaurus walking through the town or city where you live.

3

anatosaurus

30 feet long

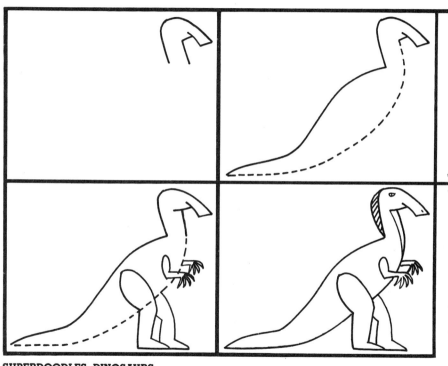

Draw an anatosaurus that is wading in a swamp, eating long, weedy plants which it has pulled up from beneath the water.

ankylosaurus

25 feet long

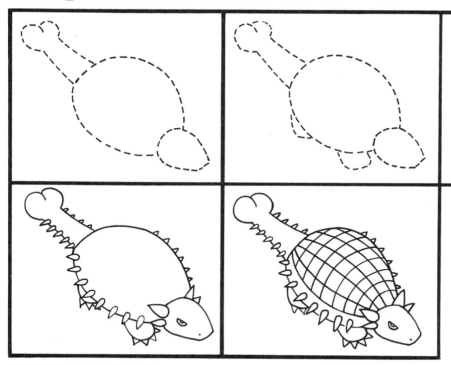

Ankylosaurus and tyrannosaurus lived in the same areas at the same time. Draw a tyrannosaurus trying to turn over an ankylosaurus.

apatosaurus

65 feet long

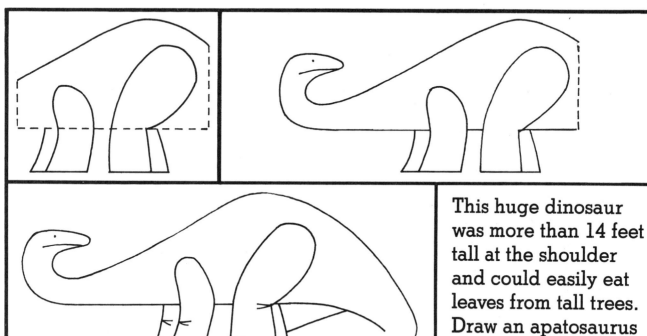

This huge dinosaur was more than 14 feet tall at the shoulder and could easily eat leaves from tall trees. Draw an apatosaurus feeding in this way.

6

brachiosaurus

80 feet long

When brachiosaurus was under water, it could breathe through an air hole on the top of its head. Draw a brachiosaurus beneath the water.

7

deinonychus

12 feet long

This dinosaur would make a good cartoon character. Draw a deinonychus that is doing something silly, weird, or awesome.

dimetrodon

10 feet long

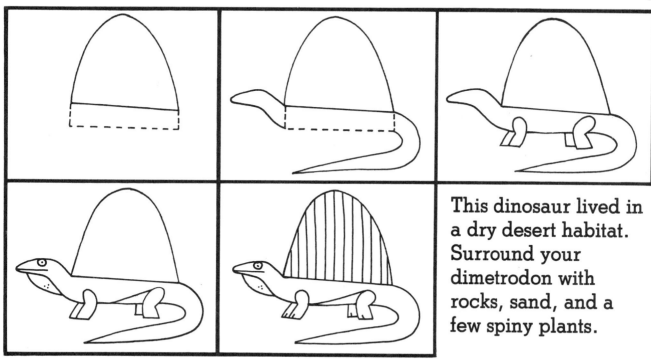

This dinosaur lived in a dry desert habitat. Surround your dimetrodon with rocks, sand, and a few spiny plants.

diplodocus

85 feet long

The long, strong tail of this dinosaur could be a powerful weapon, lashing out at other animals. Draw a diplodocus defending itself.

SUPERDOODLES: DINOSAURS
©1993—The Learning Works, Inc.

10

elasmosaurus

40 feet long

What color were the dinosaurs and other prehistoric animals? No one knows for sure. Color your elasmosaurus the way you think it should look.

11

ichthyosaurus

20 feet long

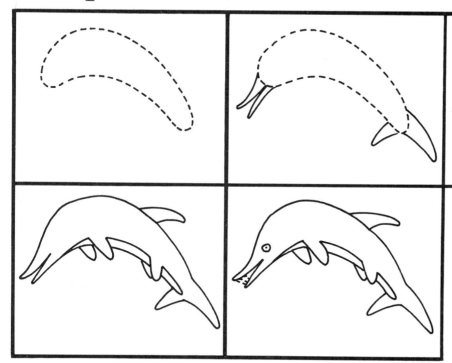

The ichthyosaurus was about half as long as an elasmosaurus. Draw some ichthyosauruses swimming past an elasmosaurus.

iguanodon

This dinosaur stood more than 16 feet tall! Draw an iguanodon chewing on the leaves of a palm tree.

kentrosaurus

15 feet long

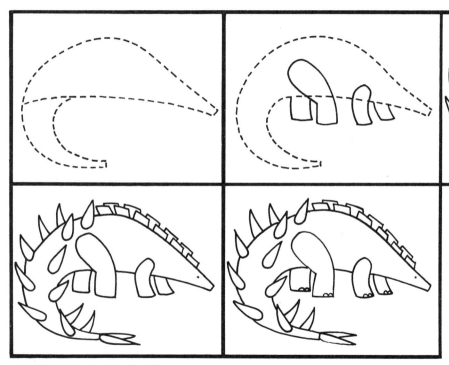

Because this reptile has plates and spikes, it looks like two kinds of dinosaurs. Draw an imaginary dinosaur that looks like two different dinosaurs.

14

lambeosaurus

50 feet long

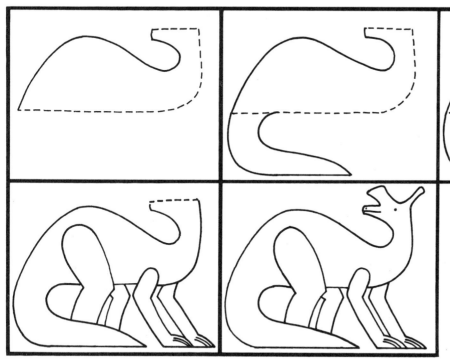

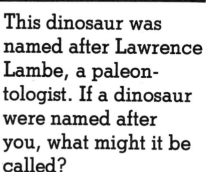

This dinosaur was named after Lawrence Lambe, a paleontologist. If a dinosaur were named after you, what might it be called?

nodosaurus

20 feet long

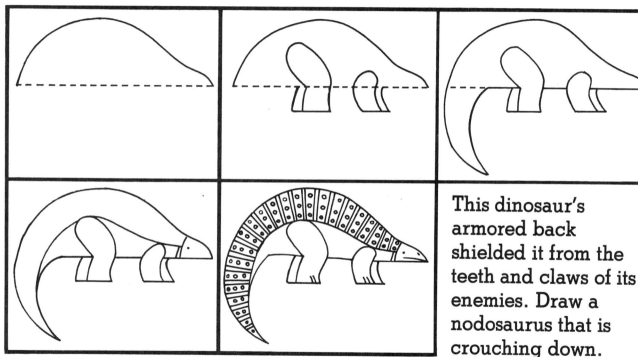

This dinosaur's armored back shielded it from the teeth and claws of its enemies. Draw a nodosaurus that is crouching down.

SUPERDOODLES: DINOSAURS
©1993—The Learning Works, Inc.

16

ouranosaurus

20 feet long

By standing sideways to the sun, ouranosaurus could absorb much warmth with its sail. Draw an ouranosaurus that is sunning itself and casting a long shadow.

oviraptor

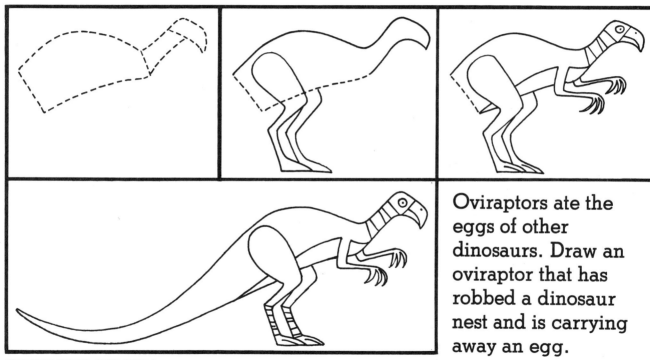

Oviraptors ate the eggs of other dinosaurs. Draw an oviraptor that has robbed a dinosaur nest and is carrying away an egg.

18

pachycephalosaurus

15 feet long

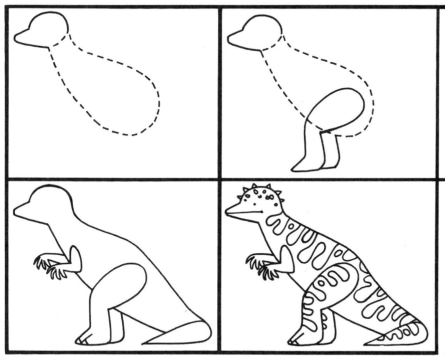

This dinosaur used the 10-inch-thick lump of bone on its head as a weapon. Draw a pachycephalosaurus using its head in a fight.

parasaurolophus

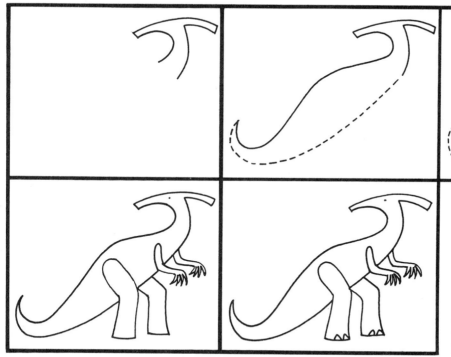

By staying in deep water, this dinosaur could protect itself from most predators. Draw a parasaurolophus that is wading in a lake.

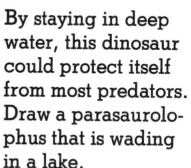

procompsognathus

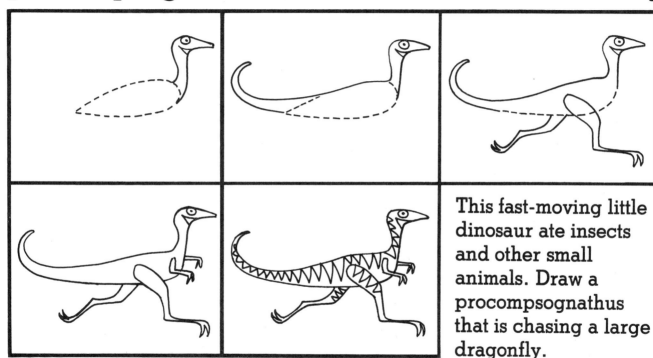

This fast-moving little dinosaur ate insects and other small animals. Draw a procompsognathus that is chasing a large dragonfly.

protoceratops

6 feet long

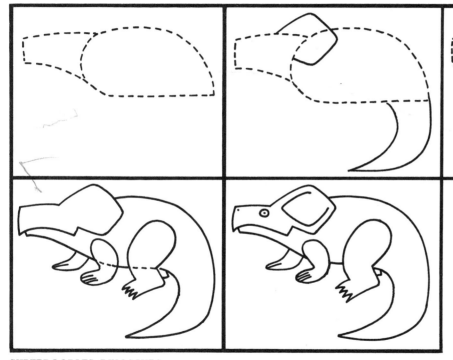

A baby protoceratops was only 12 inches long when it hatched. Draw a picture of yourself holding a baby protoceratops.

psittacosaurus

8 feet long

This dinosaur used its strong beak-like mouth to eat leaves and twigs. Draw a psittacosaurus that is feeding on a large fern.

pteranodon

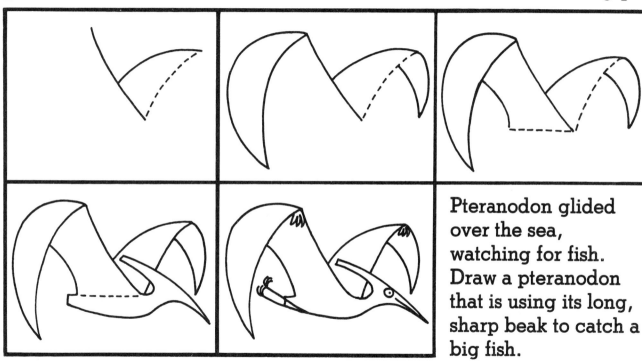

Pteranodon glided over the sea, watching for fish. Draw a pteranodon that is using its long, sharp beak to catch a big fish.

24

rhamphorhynchus

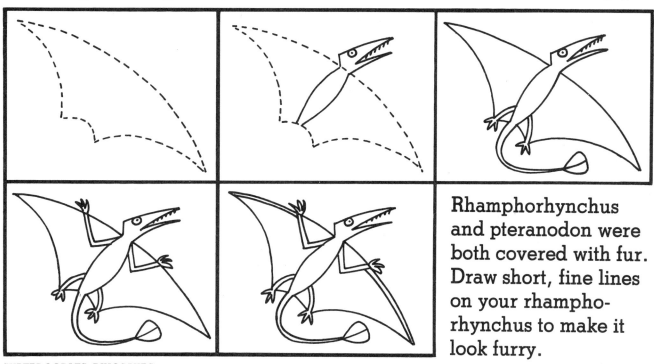

Rhamphorhynchus and pteranodon were both covered with fur. Draw short, fine lines on your rhamphorhynchus to make it look furry.

SUPERDOODLES: DINOSAURS
©1993—The Learning Works, Inc.

25

spinosaurus

40 feet long

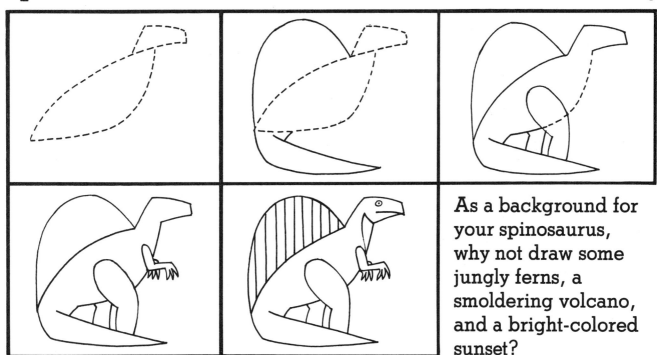

As a background for your spinosaurus, why not draw some jungly ferns, a smoldering volcano, and a bright-colored sunset?

stegosaurus

30 feet long

Rival stegosauruses probably fought for territory control. Draw two stegosauruses fighting by swinging their spiked tails at each other.

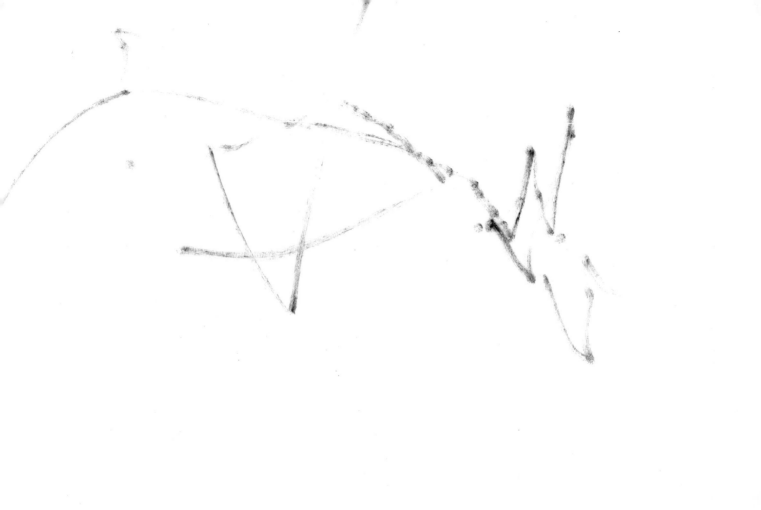

struthiomimus

12 feet long

Draw a nest of struthiomimus eggs that are beginning to hatch. Show them with shells that are cracking and babies that are peeking out.

styracosaurus

18 feet long

Draw a mother styracosaurus that is herding a small flock of babies and stands ready to defend them with the sharp spikes on her head.

SUPERDOODLES: DINOSAURS
©1993—The Learning Works, Inc.

29

torosaurus

Some torosaurus skulls were 8½ feet long. How much longer is this than your height? Draw yourself lying on the head of a torosaurus.

triceratops

35 feet long

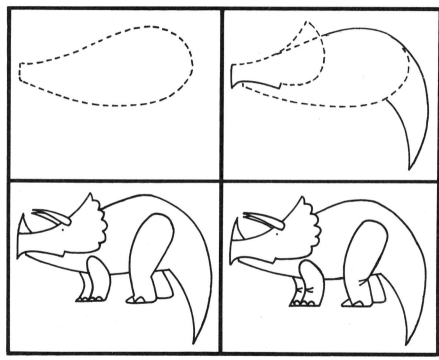

Imagine that these dinosaurs are not extinct and can be seen in zoos. Design a poster that announces a new triceratops exhibit.

tyrannosaurus

40 feet long

Tyrannosaurus teeth were 7 inches long. Draw and cut out a life-sized picture of a long, pointed tyrannosaurus tooth.